A
Word Bird
School-Day
Book

WORD BIRD'S NEW FRIEND

by Jane Belk Moncure
illustrated by Linda Hohag
color by Lori Jacobson

THE CHILD'S WORLD

MANKATO, MN

Library of Congress Cataloging in Publication Data

Moncure, Jane Belk.
    Word Bird's new friend / by Jane Belk Moncure ; illustrated by
Linda Hohag ; color by Lori Jacobson.

        p. cm. — (A Word Bird school-day book)
    Summary: When a new student arrives at school, Word Bird does his
best to help him feel at home.
    ISBN 0-89565-616-7
    [1. Schools—Fiction.   2. Animals—Fiction.]   I. Hohag, Linda,
ill.   II. Title.   III. Series: Moncure, Jane Belk.   Word Bird school
-day book.
PZ7.M739Woj   1990
[E]—dc20   90-37002

1 2 3 4 5 6 7 8 9 10 11 12 R 98 97 96 95 94 93 92 91

WORD BIRD'S
NEW FRIEND

One morning Miss Beary said,
"We have someone new in our
class. This is Little Kangaroo."
"Hi, Little Kangaroo," everyone
said. Little Kangaroo did not

say a word. He was too shy and
afraid.

"Come with me. I will show you
around," said Word Bird.

Word Bird and Little Kangaroo watched Frog work a counting puzzle.

"I cannot do that," said Little Kangaroo.

Little Kangaroo and Word Bird
watched Cat make words.

"I cannot do that," said Little
Kangaroo.

Hen and Duck were playing
store. "You can play too," they
said. But Little Kangaroo shook
his head.

Dog was making a dinosaur out
of clay. "You can make one
too," he said to Little Kangaroo.
But Little Kangaroo did not want
to play with clay.

He did not want to cut with
scissors or make things with
paste. He did not want to do
anything.

"Let's go watch Bee," said
Word Bird.

Bee was painting a picture of a
boat. "Hi, Little Kangaroo," said
Bee.

"Hi," said Little Kangaroo. "I like
boats."

"Good," said Word Bird. "I know
what we can do. We can build
a boat."

"Yes," said Little Kangaroo.
"Let's do that."

They went right to work, making
a boat with blocks.
Little Kangaroo began to smile.

13

Word Bird looked in the dress-up
box. He found two hats. "We can
be boat captains," he said.
"Let's sail around the world."

After a while, Miss Beary came
by. "My, what a fine boat," she
said. "Should we have story
time here today?"
"Yes," said Little Kangaroo.

Everyone jumped in. And Miss
Beary read them a story about
boats.

She read it two times. The
"captains" smiled.

"It's time for music," said Miss
Beary. Word Bird and Little
Kangaroo were partners. They
sat on the floor and made a
boat with their feet.

They went back and forth as
they sang, "Row, row, row your
boat," over and over.

At lunchtime, Word Bird gave
Little Kangaroo a cookie.
"Thanks, Word Bird," said Little
Kangaroo.

At recess, Word Bird and Little
Kangaroo went up and down
on the seesaw until Miss Beary
called.

"It's time for a potato-sack race," said Miss Beary. Every-one came running.

Word Bird was captain of one
team. Frog was captain of the
other. "Hop around your pole
and back again," said Miss Beary.

Away they hopped around their
poles and back again.

"Hop fast! Hop fast!" everyone
yelled.

Finally, Dog and Little Kangaroo
started out. Little Kangaroo
went hop, hop, hop very fast.

But just after he went around his pole, Little Kangaroo tripped and fell. Dog passed him by.

Word Bird helped Little
Kangaroo up. But it was too
late.

Frog's team won the race.
"It's okay," said Word Bird to
Little Kangaroo. "You hop fast.
The next time we will win."

Soon it was time to go home.
"I'll see you tomorrow," said
Word Bird.
"You bet," said Little Kangaroo.

"What did you do at school
today?" Papa asked that night.
Word Bird thought for a minute.
"I lost the potato-sack race, but
I won a friend," he said.

Can you read Word Bird's
win-a-friend words?

Be kind.
Be helpful.
Be friendly.
Smile. ☺
And you will
win friends too.